When Jessie Came
Across the Sea

For my wonderful mother
A. H.

For Patrick, Barrie, Eilís, and Caolán
with special thanks to
Kate Brennan, Owen Sharpe, and Maya Jussek
P.J. L.

ISBN 0-439-13702-0

12 11 10 9 8 7 6   4/0

Printed in the U.S.A.   08

First Scholastic printing, November 1999

This book was typeset in Bernhard Modern and Cochin Italic.
The pictures were done in watercolor and gouache.

The staff of The Jewish Museum in New York City provided generous assistance
with this book, checking both the text and the artwork for historical authenticity.

When Jessie Came Across the Sea

Amy Hest

illustrated by

P. J. Lynch

SCHOLASTIC INC.

New York Toronto London Auckland Sydney
Mexico City New Delhi Hong Kong

ONCE, IN A POOR VILLAGE FAR FROM here, there was a very small house with a slanting roof. Inside were two chairs, two narrow beds, and a table with a fine lace cloth. A potbellied stove warmed the place in winter, and warmed thin soup.

Jessie lived in that house with Grandmother. They had one skinny cow—Miss Minnie—and a patch of garden. Carrots came up here and there, and sometimes a potato.

Long ago, when Jessie was a baby, her parents died. Jessie kept her mother's wedding band, though, in a tiny silver box with a tiny lace lining. From time to time she tried it on.

In the morning, when the village boys went to the rabbi for lessons, Jessie went, too. Grandmother insisted. At night, after supper, Jessie read out loud. She practiced her letters by the fire. Grandmother sewed lace. The coins she earned were dropped in a jar on the table.

"Now, you read, Grandmother, and copy my good letters." Jessie liked being teacher.

"Me? Learn to read and write?" Grandmother scoffed.

"Sometime, you never know, you may want to read some things," Jessie said. "You may want to write."

Grandmother showed Jessie how to sew lace.

But Jessie stuck herself often. "Why do I have to learn?" she cried.

"Sometime, you never know, you may want to sew some things," Grandmother answered. "You may want to earn some money."

One evening, toward the end of summer, the rabbi called the people of the village to the synagogue. "The news from America is sad," said the rabbi. "My good brother, Mordecai, has left this world."

The villagers sighed and shook their heads. "Rest in peace," they said.

"Shortly before he died, my Mordecai sent me a ticket to America." The rabbi paused. "He wanted me to join him there."

"America! The promised land!" The voices rose as one.

"But alas!" The rabbi sighed. "I am the rabbi. How do I leave this village? How do I quit my people?" He threw up his hands. "Someone else must go in my place, someone of my choosing."

Later that night, many villagers came to the rabbi's house.

"Rabbi, listen to reason! I must go to America, for I am strong!"

"Rabbi, listen to good sense! I must go to America, for I am smart!"

"Rabbi, listen to logic! I must go to America, for I am brave!"

The rabbi listened. *How they boast and brag!* he thought. "Tonight I shall seek guidance from the Almighty," he told the villagers. "You go home. Tomorrow I will choose."

Early the next morning, Jessie and Grandmother had a caller. "I have decided," announced the rabbi. "Jessie will go to America. My brother's widow has a dress shop in New York City. Her name is Kay, and Jessie can help with the sewing. She will comfort the good lady."

Jessie's hands started to shake. *America? So far away from Grandmother!* She bit her lip, for she must not cry in front of the rabbi. *Don't make me go!* she thought.

"You know best." Grandmother spoke quietly to the rabbi. Oh, but her heart was breaking! *Dear Jessie, alone on a ship to America!* Grandmother's heart said one thing, but her head said another. Jessie must go.

A week passed quickly, then two more, as
Grandmother prepared Jessie for her journey.
The morning the ship was to sail, it rained so hard
there was no telling where the sky met the sea.
"America! Good things await you there,"
Grandmother had promised.

Jessie stood at the rail, holding her hat against
the wind and the rain. At her feet was a small
trunk, packed with a few simple clothes and layers
of lace. In Jessie's pocket was the tiny silver box
with a tiny lace lining, but her mother's wedding
band was not inside.

"Keep it safe for me, Grandmother," she had
whispered as they kissed good-bye.

"Grandmother!" she called. But the boat slipped
away from the dock, then into the channel and
on toward the sea. Umbrellas faded in the mist.
Rain pelted Jessie's face. It slid down the back
of her collar.

Later, she sat on her trunk and cried. Passengers pitied the girl with the auburn hair and ginger-colored freckles. But what could they do? Crammed together and fearful, speaking strange languages, huddling close to keep warm, what could they do for Jessie?

The ship sailed west for many days.

At first it was stormy. Jessie lay curled on a mat, too ill to eat, too ill to sleep. She thought about Grandmother in the hut with the slanting roof, eating her soup alone.

On the fourth morning the sun came up and the passengers dried out. They played cards and sang, and sometimes they argued. But mostly they talked, swapping stories and dreams. Dreams of America, where the streets were paved with gold. America, land of plenty.

Jessie began sewing to pass the time. Just to touch the soft lace was like touching Grandmother again.

A little girl with almond eyes climbed on Jessie's lap. They sang and played finger games. Then Jessie sewed lace, a tiny heart pocket for the girl's plain dress. Miss Almond Eyes danced.

An old woman came along in a tattered coat. Jessie sewed lace, a collar and cuffs, and soon that coat was grand.

A boy named Lou—he was a shoemaker's son—watched as Jessie sewed lace.

"How do you do?" he asked, tipping his hat.

Jessie smiled.

Lou took patches of leather from his splintered crate. He stitched shoes for a baby, who cried when his mother put them on his fat baby feet.

This time Jessie laughed.

Later, Lou and Jessie walked on the deck and talked. They shared black bread as the ship rolled and pitched in the wide, wide sea.

On a fine fall day they sailed past the Statue of Liberty. America! No one swapped stories or argued. Babies hushed. Even the oldest passengers, and the most seasick, stood against the rail. America!

And there it was, New York City with those tall, tall buildings that touched the sky.

Grandmother! Jessie thought.

If only you could see what I see now!

The ship docked at Ellis Island. Then papers. Wait on line. Inspections. Wait on line. Papers. Wait on line. Questions.

"What is your name?"	*"Jessie."*
"What is your age?"	*"Thirteen."*
"Are you married?"	*"No."*
"What is your occupation?"	*"I sew lace."*
"Can you read and write?"	*"Yes."*
"Are you ill?"	*"No."*

"Jessie!" A woman with bright hair burst through the crowd. "You may call me Cousin Kay." She had a soft, sweet voice and gave Jessie a hug.

Where is Lou? Jessie wondered as Cousin Kay talked on. *I forgot to say good-bye.*

Cousin Kay lived on the Lower East Side. Her house was three flights up. There was a bathtub in the kitchen, a dress shop in the parlor.

Dear Grandmother,

I miss you. Cousin Kay takes me all around the city. I wish you could see the pushcarts and shops and the trolleys speeding by. But there are too many people in America, and the streets are not gold. There are no cows. Cousin Kay bought me a pickle from a barrel. Tomorrow I begin to sew for her.

Love, Jessie

Jessie chose the yellow chair near the window in the parlor. The light was good for sewing there, and she could see the street. Best of all, Jessie liked to sew lace. A collar, cuffs, a delicate sash. Every Friday Cousin Kay gave three coins to Jessie, who dropped all three in a jar.

One afternoon, just for the fun of it, Jessie pinned a lace bodice to a plain white dress on the cutting board. She pinned lace to the sleeves.

"What a beautiful bride's dress that would be," said Cousin Kay.

Miss Emily Levy was browsing in the shop that very day. "Well, I'm getting married! Can this dress be for me?"

The wedding dress was lovely. So lovely that Emily's cousin, Miss Rachel Katz, wanted one just like it for her wedding day. Before long, brides were filling up Cousin Kay's parlor.

"You must go to school," said Cousin Kay one day. "Everyone in America speaks English. My Jessie will speak it, too." So in the morning, Jessie went to school. A Apple. B Boy. C Carrot.

This English was hard!

Dear Grandmother,

I miss you more than ever. There's a library here with rows of books. I want to read them all. On Sundays I take long walks on city streets and don't get lost anymore. There are flowers in the parks.

Love, Jessie

Jessie learned more and more English. She sewed beautiful lace. And so three years passed. She was a young lady now, sixteen.

On an icy cold Sunday in March, Jessie walked up Fifth Avenue, then into the park, where the trees were covered with new snow. Sleds crisscrossed the hills. Jessie sat on a bench and watched a young man as the wind whipped up and blew his hat off. She laughed out loud. The young man turned. *Lou!* Jessie couldn't believe her eyes. *Lou, her friend from the ship!* Jessie waved. And Lou, the shoemaker's son, waved back. He would have tipped his hat, but it was far away.

The next Sunday they met again on the bench in the park. And the Sunday after that.

Dear Grandmother,

I have a special friend. He makes good strong shoes from patches of leather. His name is Lou. You will like him, Grandmother. I promise.

Love, Jessie

One evening Jessie met Lou's parents, his brother, and his three sisters. She brought a basket of bread with a lace cloth. The two littlest sisters cried when she left.

"Marry me?" asked Lou, on the stairs outside his house.

"Soon." Jessie smiled and held his hand.

Days passed, and weeks. Jessie sewed lace, early and late. Months went by. Jessie sewed and sewed, and then one day the jar was filled with coins. She brought it to a man who sold tickets to America. "I need a ticket for Grandmother," she said.

Every day, Jessie rushed down three flights of stairs to the mailbox. The letter came, finally, on a breezy day. The handwriting was shaky, but Jessie knew Grandmother had written every word herself.

Dear Jessie,

I sewed the ticket to the lining of my coat.
I say goodbye to this village.
The rabbi is taking Miss Minnie.

Your loving Grandmother

The morning her ship arrived in New York
Harbor, it rained so hard there was no telling
where the sky met the sea. Grandmother was older
than Jessie remembered, and much more frail.
They held each other for a long time.

"I've brought something for you," Grandmother
whispered, "from across the sea."

With that, she slipped Jessie's mother's wedding
band into Jessie's hand.

Then they went home, for there was
going to be a wedding.